MW00909983

Presented To:

_____

Date:

_____

Little Girls Book of Prayers for Toddlers

Copyright © 2002 Carolyn Larsen and illistrator Caron Turk

Published by New Kids Media™ in association with Baker Books, a division of Baker Book House Company, P.O. Box 6287, Grand Rapids, MI 49516-6287

Printed in China.

ISBN 0-8010-4500-2

For current information about all releases from Baker Book House, visit our web site:

http://www.bakerbooks.com

Little Girls Book of Prayers For Toddlers

Carolyn Larsen
Illustrated by Caron Turk

BAKER
A DIVISION OF
Baker Book House Co

Dear God,

You made sunshine. You made soft grass. You made fluffy clouds, and you made me! Thank you, God, for making me.

Amen

God loves me...this I know...the Bible tells me so.

Dear God,

Sometimes I feel happy. Sometimes I feel sad. But you love me no matter what. Thank you for loving me.

Amen

5

Dear God,

It's time for bed. Thank you for a good day and thank you for nighttime. Please watch over me while I sleep.

Amen

God can do anything.

Dear God,

How did you think of so many things to make? How do you keep the sun in the sky? How did you think of butterflies? You did a good job, God.

Amen

Dear God,

Thank you for my nice bed. Thank you for books to read. Thank you, God, for everything!

Amen

Dear God,

Pets are a good idea. My pet loves me and I love him. Thank you, God, for pets.

Amen

Dear God,

I like walking with my mom and dad. They hold my hands and swing me over the snow. Thank you for Mommy and Daddy.

Amen

Dear God,

I have the best mom in the world. She plays with me and reads with me. Sometimes we eat ice cream in the backyard. Thank you for my mom.

Amen

Dear God,

My daddy is the best. He plays with me. He fixes things that are broken. He reads me stories. Thank you for my daddy.

Amen

I love my daddy ♥ He loves me a lot ♥ We dance all around the room ♥ We like to sing ♥ We like to laugh ♥

Dear God,

I love my family. Mommy and Daddy take good care of me. My brothers and sisters play with me. Thank you for my family!

Amen

Dear God,

I love snow. Sometimes Daddy and Mommy pull me on my sled. Sometimes we make a snowman. Sometimes we make snow ice cream —yum! Thank you for snow.

Amen

Dear God,

I love my grandma and grandpa.
Sometimes they take me on trips.
Sometimes we do fun things together at
home. Please take good care of them.

Amen

Dear God,

Yippee! Jesus is alive! Thank you for Jesus.
I know that you love me. I love you too.

Amen

Dear God,

It's Christmas! I love our Christmas tree, all the presents, the songs, and the cookies that we decorate. Most of all I like singing "Happy Birthday, Jesus!"

Amen

Dear God,

Mommy and I like to look at the clouds. Sometimes they look like puppies, then they change and look like fish. Thank you for making cloud pictures.

Amen

Dear God,

Thank you for sunshine. It makes my skin feel nice and warm. When I'm sad sunshine cheers me up. Sunshine was a good idea.

Amen

Dear God,

My friend and I played in the rain today. We splashed in puddles. We made leaves into boats. It was fun. Thank you for rain showers.

Amen

Dear God,

I saw a rainbow today. It was red and yellow and purple and orange. Mommy says a rainbow is supposed to remind me of you. It did.

Amen

Dear God,

Mommy and Daddy read Bible stories to me every night. Then we pray together. Thank you for hearing our prayers. Thank you for answering them.

Amen

Dear God,

My house is safe and warm and a good place
to be when it's rainy outside. It has lots of love
inside it too. Thank you for my house.

Amen

Dear God,

Wow! Look at all the stars. They fill up the sky so it isn't black and empty. Was it fun to put them in the sky? It's fun to look at them. Thank you for the stars.

Amen

Dear God,

Mommy says that if you lined up all the little girls in the world and let her choose any one she wanted . . . she would choose me!
I love Mommy.

Amen

Dear God,

My grandpa is sick. Would you please help him feel better? I'd like that 'cause I love my grandpa.

Amen

Dear God,

I don't like it when it's stormy. When the sky is dark and the wind blows hard, I get scared. I'm glad to know that you will take care of me.

Amen

Dear God,

My throat is scratchy, my head hurts, and I don't feel good. Thank you that Mommy and Daddy take good care of me. Could you please help me feel better? Thank you.

Amen

Dear God,

Mommy and Daddy work so hard to take care of our family. But they still take time to read and pray with me every night. Take care of my mommy and daddy.

Amen

Dear God,

I have to go to the hospital and I'm kind of scared. Mommy says the doctors will take good care of me. She and Daddy will stay with me. Best of all, she says you will be with me too. Thanks.

Amen

Dear God,

I love the stories Mommy reads me about Jesus. First he was a little baby. Then he grew up and made sick people well. I love Jesus.

Amen

Now Write Your Own Prayer

Dear God,

_____

_____

_____

Amen